# Bob the Builder™

# Bob's Birthday

based on the script by
**Diane Redmond**

with thanks to
**Hot Animation**

Simon Spotlight

New York    London    Toronto    Sydney    Singapore

Based upon the television series *Bob the Builder*™ created by HIT Entertainment PLC
and Keith Chapman, with thanks to HOT Animation, as seen on Nick Jr.®

SIMON SPOTLIGHT
An imprint of Simon & Schuster Children's Publishing Division
1230 Avenue of the Americas
New York, New York 10020

Manufactured in the United States of America

4  6  8  10  9  7  5

ISBN 0-689-84545-6

"Listen, everybody!" Wendy exclaimed. "Today is Bob's birthday. Let's pretend it's just an ordinary day and surprise Bob with a party tonight!"

"Won't Bob be disappointed if we don't wish him a happy birthday?" asked Muck.

"We can wish him a happy birthday at the party," Wendy explained. "Now remember, it's a secret. Not a word to Bob!"

Just then Bob came into the yard.

"Hi, Wendy, was there any mail for me?" he asked.

"Were you expecting anything special?"

"Uh . . . no. Nothing special," he said.

He turned to Scoop and Lofty. "We have to go and fix Farmer Pickles's barn."
"Have a good day, Bob," Wendy called.
"I'll try," mumbled Bob as he rolled out of the yard with Scoop and Lofty.
Wendy sighed. "Now I can begin baking Bob's birthday cake!"

When Bob, Scoop, and Lofty got to Farmer Pickles's barn, Travis and Spud were already there. Bob started to pull the old planking off the wall so he could replace it with new planking.

"Pull harder, Bob!" yelled Spud.

"I'm doing my best," grunted Bob. Suddenly the plank came loose and Bob fell back on his bottom.

Things weren't going that well for Bob on his birthday!

Back at the yard Dizzy and Muck watched Wendy make Bob's birthday cake. "Cake mixing looks easy," said Dizzy. "You just throw everything together and mix it up. Just like making concrete!"

"Hey, why don't we make Bob a concrete cake he can keep forever? **Can we make it?**" asked Muck.

"**Yes, we can!**" exclaimed Dizzy.

Dizzy whipped up a load of her very best concrete. Then she poured it into a tire mold.

Then Roley helped Muck and Dizzy decorate their concrete
cake with some flowers, feathers, and leaves.
  "Wow! Cool cake," Roley said.

At Farmer Pickles's barn Bob and Lofty were still working hard. Their work was coming along nicely.

"Travis and Spud, aren't you two supposed to be delivering Farmer Pickles's eggs?" asked Bob.

"You're right!" said Travis, starting up his engine. "Come on, Spud," he called. "I'll drop you off at Bob's house."

At Bob's house, Wendy was done making Bob's birthday cake. "Mmmmmm!" exclaimed Spud as he scooped some icing off the cake and plopped it into his mouth.

"Spud!" Wendy yelled.

"I'm sorry, Wendy," Spud mumbled. "But it looks so good!"

"Do you want to help me put the candles on the cake?" asked Wendy.

"You bet! Spud's on the job!" he laughed.

As Bob nailed the last plank into Farmer Pickles's barn, his cell phone rang. "Maybe this is a birthday phone call," he said hopefully. It was Wendy. "Hi, Bob," she said. "When are you coming home?"

"Actually we've just finished and we are on our way," Bob told her. "Why . . . any special reason?"

"No," Wendy replied. "I've just got a few letters for you to sign. Bye."

"No 'Happy Birthday, Bob'," Bob murmured to himself.

Scoop winked at Lofty. "Come on, Bob. Time to go home!" he said.

Back at the yard Wendy, Muck, Dizzy, and Roley had
decorated a table and covered it with cakes and presents.
Bob couldn't believe his eyes when he arrived back at the yard.

"Surprise!" laughed Wendy.
"I thought you forgot my birthday!" Bob exclaimed.
"Forget your birthday?" Wendy teased. "Never! Look! You've got two cakes—a real cake to eat and a concrete cake you can keep forever!"

Everybody burst out singing:

"Bob the Builder, it's his birthday!
Bob the Builder, yes, it is!
It's Bob's birthday, can we sing it?
It's Bob's birthday—yes, we can!"

"And don't forget your mail!" Wendy said.
"All these birthday cards for me?" gasped Bob.
"Of course," replied Wendy, "you're the Birthday Builder!"
Everyone cheered, "Hooray!"

"Now can I please have a slice of that yummy-looking cake?" begged Spud, interrupting.

"Of course you may," said Bob as he cut Spud a huge piece.

Spud stuffed the piece of cake into his mouth and smiled.
"Like I always say: 'I'm on the job, Bob!'"